REEM: INTO THE UNKNOWN

AHMED SALAH AL-MAHDI

CONTENTS

DEDICATION

To my grandmother: Because it was her tales, told to me when I was still small, that first drew me to these magical worlds of make-believe.

To my mother: Because she was the first to instill in me the love of reading, giving me my first book when I was young.

To my father: Because his small library made me realize that reading is not just entering another world, but rather entering a never-ending procession of worlds.

To my brothers Muhammad, Jihad, and Mahmoud: for their endless support.

To all my friends and first readers: Without your criticism of my work, I would not be where I am now.

Finally, I dedicate this to Farah, Safiya and Farida, who brought never-ending joy and pleasure to my life. To you, children that you are, I dedicate this book.

Special thanks to: Melanie Autumn Magidow, Marcia Lynx Qualey, Emad El-Din Aysha, and Blaze Ward for their suggestions and support, and to David Garcia Forés for the cover art.

1

JUST ANOTHER DAY

In his office at one of Egypt's biggest companies, Saif sat in front of his computer's bright screen, feeling totally bored. He stared absentmindedly at the numbers that ran past on his screen, and from time to time he yawned and checked the wooden clock that hung on the wall, wondering how much time was left till the workday ended. Although he had a digital clock in the corner of his screen, he preferred the sound of the wooden clock ticking away, with its constant, circular, clockwise movement, which gave him a sense of the passage of time.

He struck the keys with the rapid movements that now came naturally to him, as he was used to the mundane work that drained away hours of his life each day. He felt especially weary today, because it was the last day of the week, and he was looking forward to the weekend. It seemed there was an unwritten rule that, the closer the thing you wanted, the more you craved it. He didn't actually do much on the weekends — just watch TV and read the occasional novel — as he lived alone, and he preferred not to hang out much with his friends, who'd become used to his retiring personality.

Saif glanced up again at the wooden clock and noticed there were only about fifteen minutes remaining, so he arranged the papers on his desk and shut down his computer. Once the clock struck three, he left the office and rushed down the stairs. He didn't like the elevator, since he was claustrophobic. Once he reached the ground floor, he headed to the garage, looking around for his car, trying to remember where he'd parked it that morning. Finally he found the car and rushed toward it.

The garage worker was waving as usual to greet him, so he waved back before he got into his car. He started up the engine, which roared as it always did. Then he left the office building, driving the car into the crowded city streets, heading straight for home. To pass the time, he began to think about what he'd have for lunch — although he didn't need to worry about *deciding* what to eat, since he lived alone. He might get some take-away, or cook a simple meal using his humble culinary skills, which hadn't improved, even though he'd lived alone for many years. Today was, as he always told himself, "just another day."

Yet on *this* particular day, there was construction work on the main road, and drivers had a hard time trying to pass through the tiny sliver of road that barely allowed a single car to edge through. Saif wasn't the kind of person who could bear sitting in a Cairo traffic jam, so he decided to take another route home. This way was actually longer, forcing him to take several side roads, but for him it was still better than being stuck with all the angry drivers on the main road.

When Saif passed a fast-food restaurant, he seized the

opportunity and bought some hot sandwiches to eat on the long ride home. But then, before he got home, he noticed a pet store. Even though it was close to his apartment, this was the first time he'd seen it. If he hadn't been forced to change his daily route, he might never have run across the shop.

He felt a sudden desire for a pet, without knowing where the urge had come from. Maybe it was just the idea of doing something new and different, or maybe it was because his friends kept insisting that he marry, telling him that living alone could make him lose his mind. Maybe the company of a pet would relieve his loneliness. Although the idea seemed strange to him at first, after he turned it over in his head – while he was standing in front of the shop – he said to himself, "Why not?"

Once he'd entered the store, the shop owner approached him. "Welcome to my shop, Sir. Are you looking for something in particular?"

"I don't have anything specific in mind," Saif said as he looked around. "I was just thinking in general about getting a pet. I haven't decided what sort of animal I want to get."

The shop owner nodded; he'd had this sort of customer before. Usually they took a look around and then left, so the owner let Saif wander around the shop.

Saif moved around the shop, looking at the different pets. There were the ordinary pets such as cats, dogs, birds, and goldfish, and then there were the odd ones, like chameleons and snakes. He also saw some strange creatures, of the sort he'd only seen on the National Geographic channel, which he always liked to watch.

He kept on walking among the cages with clear curiosity and fascination—seeing these animals in vibrant real life was very different from watching them on the cold glass of TV.

While Saif was lost in his thoughts, trying to decide which pet to buy, he noticed a cage covered with a black swath of cloth, as if to conceal whatever lay inside. It aroused his curiosity, so he approached the cage, wondering what might be inside, and why the shop owner would've hidden it. He hesitated a bit as he reached for the black cover, slowly revealing what lay beneath. Once it was uncovered, he heard a loud hissing and saw an ugly black cat, arching its back while opening its mouth to reveal its fangs, all while it kept up its hostile hissing.

After hearing the sound, the shop owner rushed toward him and covered the cage with the black cloth. Nonetheless, the cat kept on meowing and hissing, and the shop owner seemed troubled.

"I only took the cover off the cage to see what was inside," Saif said, defending himself. "The black cat really startled me."

"Excuse me, Sir." The shop owner sighed. "That's why I had it covered, because it scares the customers."

Curiosity was growing inside Saif. "So why would you keep such a weird cat in your shop?"

The owner paused a little, then said, "I've had this cat for a long time, and no one's wanted to buy it. People are superstitious about black cats—they think they're a bad omen. So I covered the cage, since I was afraid it might drive the customers away."

"Why not just get rid of it?" Saif asked, puzzled.

The shop owner avoided making eye contact with Saif. "I can't."

Saif felt sorry for the cat—he thought about how it was as lonely as he was. Then a crazy idea popped into his mind, although it seemed reasonable to him in the moment. "I'll buy this cat," he said, excited.

The shop owner looked exultant to hear it. At first, it looked as if he couldn't believe his ears, and the price he gave for the cat was a pittance. He even threw in the carrying cage as a gift. Saif also bought some canned cat food from the shop. Then he left the shop, heading for his car, and put the cage on the passenger seat. He sat at the wheel, started the car, and resumed the journey home.

It wasn't long before Saif arrived, parking his car in the garage. He carried the cage up with him, heading towards the front door, stepping inside, flipping on the light switches.

"I hope you'll get used to this place right away," Saif said, setting the cage down on the floor and letting out the cat. "It's your home now."

The cat showed no reaction, save for slowly stepping out of the cage and gazing at Saif with cold eyes, which made him nervous. He didn't know what to do. It was his first experience taking care of an animal at home.

"You must be hungry," he said. "I'll change, and then I'll get you something to eat."

Saif left the cat and went up to the second floor, where his bedroom was, to change and rest his tired limbs a little. He saw the cat in the mirror as he went back down, still changing his clothes. He stepped into the room and found it giving him a fixed stare. The cold gaze of this black cat sent shivers down his spine. He felt nervous as he approached the cat, trying to reach down and pet him.

"Don't freak out," he said to himself. "It's just a normal cat."

But as soon as his hand got near the cat, it hissed and arched its back. Saif quickly pulled his hand away. "No problem, it's our first day together," he said nervously. "We'll get used to each other in no time."

When he went to the kitchen, the cat followed him with steady steps, watching as Saif opened a tin of cat food and placed the food in a plastic dish. He put the dish in front of the cat while saying, "Cute cat."

Up in his bedroom, Saif lay on the bed, reading a novel that he'd started a few days ago and hadn't yet finished. He was about to doze off, but he wanted to finish a chapter or two before going to bed. He turned the pages, bored, wondering if he should pick up another novel. At just this moment, the cat entered the room meowing. He tried to ignore it and keep reading, but the cat's cold stares made him uncomfortable. He put the novel aside, got up from the bed, shooed the cat out of the room, and got back to the novel. But he couldn't concentrate because the cat kept insistently scratching at the door. He sighed. "It seems like the cat is a little *too* friendly," he said sarcastically.

He got up, opened the door, lifted up the cat, and placed it on the bed. "I hope you're comfortable now."

Now he couldn't focus on the novel at all. He looked at the cat as it yawned and stretched its body. It did a few circles in place before it put its head down between its front legs. Saif watched it and pondered all that had happened that day. Then he felt his consciousness calmly withdraw as he, in turn, fell asleep.

The next morning, Saif woke to the feeling of hot breath striking his face. He opened his eyes to find the black cat sitting next to his head, looking down at him.

Saif jumped off the bed in panic, then remembered that he'd bought the cat yesterday. *It'll just take some time to get used to having a cat around the house.*

He went to the bathroom to have a quick shower, then headed to the kitchen to prepare his usual breakfast, which was mostly made up of eggs, cheese, and a hot cup of milk. This time, he poured some milk in a small dish for the cat, and it licked the dish in satisfaction.

It was the weekend, which meant Saif didn't have to go to the work, so he spent the day doing laundry, washing the dishes, pruning the garden, mowing the lawn, and other tasks that a single man who lived alone in the suburbs had to do. At the same time, he had to ignore the stares of the cat as it followed him all over the place, which was the most difficult task of all.

In the afternoon, he had lunch, and then he sat on the couch in the living room to watch some TV.

He flipped through the channels, looking for something entertaining to watch. As he did, the cat crouched on the living room floor, staring at the TV screen. But the cat seemed to grow weary of it, and so it put its head between its feet. Seeing that the cat had fallen asleep, Saif climbed to the second floor to finish some overdue work on his computer. He closed the door behind him, sat at the desk, and set to work. He kept at it for a while before he suddenly noticed the sound of meowing and claws scratching at the wooden door. He ignored the sound, trying to concentrate on his work, but the cat's mewling made him lose his temper. "Meow all you like, I won't open the door this time!"

The sound of meowing and clawing went on for a while. Then it stopped. Silence reigned. Saif sighed in relief and got back to his work. Suddenly, he heard a swishing sound coming from outside the window. He looked toward it, and then he jumped out of his seat when he saw the black cat standing at the windowsill, looking at him with a fixed cold stare. Behind it, moonlight slipped into the room.

Saif had reached his breaking point; he was sure now that the cat was not at all normal. He made a decision: he'd take the cat back to the shop where he'd bought it. In a few minutes, he'd changed his clothes, picked up the cat – which kept on meowing and scratching his hand – put it in the cage, and left the house. The shop wasn't far from his house, so he decided not to get his car out of the garage. Instead, he'd walk to the pet store. As he set eyes on the store, he saw the shop owner preparing to close up. "Hey!" Saif yelled, rushing toward him.

The man turned toward Saif and saw him carrying the black cat. He frowned. "How may I help you, Sir?" he asked in a hostile tone.

"I want to return this cat," Saif said impatiently.

"Unfortunately, Sir," the shop owner said with a firm shake of his head, "no returns or replacements. That's store policy."

Saif was disappointed. He tried to bargain with the shop owner, but the man seemed very determined. Saif even offering to return the cat without getting his money back, but the shop owner was adamant: *no returns*. Saif sighed angrily, walked away from the store, and headed toward his house.

Night had fallen. The streets were dark, except for the glow from a few lampposts that cast more shadow than light. He walked in the quiet streets without paying attention to the few passers-by who looked at him, wondering why he was carrying a cage with a cat in it.

After a while, the passers-by became fewer and fewer, until he found himself alone in the dark, quiet streets. Suddenly an idea struck him. It was crazy, but he liked it. "Why not?" he said to himself.

He looked around to make sure that no one was watching him, and then he turned into one of the dark alleys and opened the cage. "Go!" he said to the cat.

The black cat came out of the cage, walked a few steps away, and then looked at Saif. "Go away and never come back!" Saif said, an edge of threat in his voice.

The cat didn't seem to understand what was being said, and it continued to look at him without moving.

Saif left him, heading home. Every once in a while, he looked back to make sure the cat wasn't following him. Finally, he reached home, climbed to the second floor, and, exhausted, threw his body down on the bed. In no time at all, he was sound asleep.

THE MYSTERY OF THE BLACK CAT

Saif was racing down a narrow street, his breaths heavy and his movements slow, in spite of his desperate attempts to flee. The black cat was behind him; it had grown dozens of sizes larger, to the point that it was bigger now than Saif, meowing and chasing him down this tight street. Suddenly, the cat's eyes grew so quickly that they swallowed Saif whole. He tried to scream as he fell into the huge eyes, but he felt his voice being muffled. He woke from his nightmare all at once, unable to breathe. To his shock, he found the black cat crouched on his face, covering his mouth and nose with its thick black fur. In the dim light coming from the window, the cat was so frightening that Saif screamed in horror. He tried to the get the cat off his face, but it held onto his flesh with its claws. He pulled it so hard that it raked gashes into his face before he managed to throw it into a corner of the room. The cat yowled in rage when it hit the floor, and Saif's face burned with pain. *How on earth was the cat able to get back in the house?* There was something unnatural about this cat. He remembered how the pet-shop owner had been so happy to get rid of it. Now Saif was sure it wasn't because the cat was black or ugly. There was another reason, something the shop owner hadn't told him. He looked at the cat, which was licking its paws and staring back at Saif with its cold eyes. "What curse have I brought upon myself?" he asked, staring at the cat in revulsion. He lost any desire to go back to sleep.

He looked through the window at the faint light of dawn and decided to go to the pet store once again and interrogate the shop owner about this mysterious cat. He needed to know its story, whatever the cost. But first, he went to the bathroom to put some bandages on the wounds that had been inscribed onto his face by the cat's claws. He thought for a moment of having breakfast, but he had no real appetite for food at that moment, so he settled for a cup of coffee to help him regain his focus.

Once the first sunray had snuck into his room, he changed his clothes and went downstairs. He remembered that he'd left the cat's cage in a side street, so he put the cat into a wooden box instead. He heard it clawing the insides of the box in a rage, but he ignored it as headed toward the car. Once there, he put the box on the passenger seat. The roaring of the engine broke the morning's silence as he drove through the city's now quiet streets. He reached the store in a few minutes and found it still closed; he looked at his watch and saw that it was not yet six o'clock. He'd come too early, and now he would have to wait.

Saif busied himself with observing the surroundings—it was very early in the morning, and everything was covered in a soft mist. Dew condensed on the leaves of the trees that decorated the street, and also on the glass windows of the cars. The cat kept on scratching at the wooden box, meowing in rage. The long wait, along with the sound of the meowing and scratching and the foggy weather, made Saif lose his temper. "Shut up, God damn it!" he shouted fiercely.

Minutes passed like hours. He wanted to be done with this matter as quickly as possible. He checked his watch every few minutes to see how much time had passed as he waited for the shop owner. After nearly an hour, he saw the man approaching the store with steady steps. Saif watched him from a distance as he opened the store's front doors. Then Saif got out of the car, leaving the wooden box in it. He closed his door and approached the store alone.

The shop owner startled with recognition as Saif said, "Good morning."

The man turned around abruptly, ready to throw him out, but then he saw Saif's wounded face, tired from too much thinking and lack of sleep, covered by bandages. His expression dropped into confusion. "You again?" he said nervously. "I told you that there is no return or replace—"

Recent events, combined with a lack of sleep and racing thoughts, had driven Saif half-crazy. He leaned over the shop owner, furious, and seized his clothes. "Listen!" he said. "Yesterday I tried to get rid of this damn cat, but it came back again, somehow, and tried to kill me! Today, you're going to take it back no matter what."

Fear spread across the shop owner's face. He could see that Saif was in a precarious state of mind, and clearly feared he might do something irrational. He tried to pull himself out of Saif's grasp. "Please, I don't want it back," he said, defending himself. "That cat almost drove me crazy. And even if I took it back, how could you be sure it won't get back to you all over again? I didn't sell you the cat on purpose. It was your choice, and I am not responsible!"

The shop owner's words broke through Saif's fury, and he calmed down a little. "There's a mystery around this cat, and I can tell you know something. Why don't you just come clean and tell me everything you know?"

"I swear to you, Sir, I don't know what you're talking about," the shop owner said, his voice pleading. "I bought this cat cheap, but I couldn't sell it. Every customer who came in and saw it didn't like it. I tried to get rid of the cat several times, but *every* time it came back. There's something wicked about this cat, but I don't know what it is!"

Saif loosened his grip on the front of the shop owner's clothes. "So it's true," he whispered, as if to himself. "I'm not imagining things."

Yet what the shop owner had told him only increased his bewilderment about the mystery of the cat. Saif turned again toward the shop owner, who raised his arm in front of his face to protect himself.

"I want you to tell me everything about how you got this cat," Saif ordered. "From the very beginning."

"I remember it…that horrid day when I bought the cat." The shop owner looked as though he were searching his memory. "It started like any other day. I was sitting in the store, minding my own business, when a little girl came in, carrying the cat in her arms. She offered to sell it for almost nothing, but she seemed sad about it. She told me the cat was dear to her, but that she needed the money. I hesitated at first, wondering if I should really buy the cat, but the price made me do it. Besides, the little girl was so insistent about selling the cat, I just gave her the money and bought the thing."

Saif felt he finally had a lead on this strange case. "Do you know anything about the girl? Her name, her address, any information that might lead me to her?" He looked intently at the shop owner.

The man gave his head a regretful shake. "Unfortunately, that was the only time I saw her."

Saif sighed in distress. Then, curious: "Do you remember what she was wearing that day?"

The shop owner thought for a while. "She was wearing a white dress. And she looked poor."

Saif pressed a hand to his forehead as he thought. "She's a little girl, so she must live near here. Maybe I can ask about her in the neighborhood."

"An excellent idea!" the shop owner said eagerly. Clearly, all he wanted was to get rid of Saif, and he would happily approve *any* idea that helped him get Saif out of the store. Then another idea struck the owner. "You could ask about her in the market, since she seemed to be of modest means. The people at the market are simple folk, and they usually know each other. You could start your search there."

"Yes, that's probably a good idea," Saif said, unaware that all the shop owner wanted was to keep him as far as possible from the store.

He left the store in a hurry after the pet-shop owner wished him good luck. The man kept his eyes trained on Saif as he left. In the end, he sighed in relief. "What a way to start the day!"

Saif went back to his car and looked at the wooden box. He heard the usual sounds of mewing and scratching, but he ignored it, turning over the car engine so he could hear the machine growl once again in the calm morning. He drove through the calm, misty streets, feeling a lovely chill and thinking about his quest to find the little girl. It sounded silly to ask people about a little girl in a white dress, but there was no other way.

Thoughts circled each other in his mind. Who was this girl? What was the secret behind the black cat? What was really going on? He kept on thinking until he reached the local market. He hesitated, imagining himself asking about a little girl and a black cat! Even though it seemed ridiculous, he told himself there was no other way to find out about the girl. The market was the only place where he could get information, for the vendors there knew each other and dealt with most of the people who lived nearby. Surely he would find *something*. That's what he said, both to encourage himself and to relieve a little of his stress.

He pulled the cat out of the box. For some reason, it had grown calm and didn't try to scratch his hand with its claws. Saif felt uneasy with the sudden calmness. "What are you hiding, you devil?"

Then he stepped out of the car and slammed the door. He was holding the cat and thinking about where to begin his search. It was still early. The shop owners were still sorting out their goods, and there weren't many customers. He started asking the shop owners, especially the old ones, if they had ever seen a girl in a white dress holding a black cat. The answer was always no, no one had ever seen her, or some said they might have seen her and forgotten, since the vendors dealt with dozens of people every day, men and women and kids, and maybe the girl had passed them by, but they couldn't remember her. After an hour, Saif lost all hope of finding the girl. "I was chasing a ghost all along," he muttered to himself.

His search led him to the end of the market, where the river crossed at the edge of the city. He looked out at the landscape of green trees and dewy blades of grass that grew on the banks of the river, and he felt tired from the long walk and the constant asking. So he lay down on the green, grassy ground under the shadow of a lush green tree, setting the black cat beside him. He breathed deeply of the fresh air, enjoying the cool breeze blowing up from the river. By that time, the sun's intensity had increased, which made him want to stay in the cold air in the lovely shade of the tree. The black cat stretched out and put its head on its pawns, wrapping its tail around its body. It looked as if it had fallen asleep.

The minutes passed as Saif hung in this state, swinging between wakefulness and sleep. Then he noticed a little boy staring at him from far off with a strange expression on his face. At that moment, Saif realized that he'd spotted the boy in the market a few times already, and he wondered if the boy was following him. He called out to the boy, who came closer with hesitant steps. Saif looked the boy up and down: he was no more than twelve years old and wearing simple, modest clothes. "Who are you, kid, and why are you following me?" he asked.

"I want to know how you got this cat," the boy said sharply. "And why are you asking about the girl?"

Saif was surprised by the boy's cutting question. "And why do you care?"

The boy hesitated.

"Well, you seem to know something," Saif said, trying to encourage the boy to speak.

The boy gave a miserable sigh. "Yes, I know the girl you're looking for."

3

THE GIRL IN WHITE

Osama was a boy of twelve. Since his father's death many years before, he'd lived alone with his mother, who was solely responsible for his upbringing and education. In order to make a living, his mother worked as a vendor in the market that stood near the river, at the very edge of the city. In the past, he'd gone to the market with his mother on the weekends. But Osama wasn't gifted at dealing with people, and he didn't like the overcrowding of the market, the voices selling and buying, bargaining over prices, and all the other chatter. So he would walk toward the quiet river and enjoy the sight of the green trees on the other bank, his soul gravitating towards the calm of nature. With time, he grew used to crossing the small bridge at the end of the market and heading to the other side, where he spent most of his time observing nature and letting his mind wander. Sometimes, he created simple games that he could play alone as he waited for his mother to finish selling the vegetables and fruits that she'd brought with her. Then they would return to their home, which wasn't far from the market.

One day, as he was playing in the woods as usual, trying to invent some new game, Osama saw a young girl about his age, wearing a simple white dress, blushing and looking at him in surprise. Rays of sunlight snuck through the tree branches and reflected off her golden hair. Her eyes were as blue as the river, and she was the most beautiful girl he had ever seen. Before he opened his mouth to speak, she ran away through the trees. He watched in astonishment, wondering about this young girl who he had never seen before.

He stood there, bewildered and rooted in place, as the girl disappeared among the trees. He hesitated before he followed her into the woods, asking, "Who are you?" He had never gone very far into the tangled brush, so he was afraid he might get lost. He decided to go back before his mother began to worry.

"What's the matter, Osama?" his mom asked, concerned, when she saw the look on his face.

"Nothing," he muttered, shaking his head.

His mother wasn't convinced by his answer, but she preferred not to press him. "I hope everything is okay, my sweet son," she said. "I'll make us some dinner."

After dinner, Osama went to his room and lay on his bed, thinking about the girl in the white dress. "I wonder who she is!" Her face wasn't familiar, and he was sure he hadn't seen her before. He also wondered why she'd been there alone among the trees. He sank deeper and deeper into these thoughts until he fell asleep.

He woke the next morning, eager to go to the market, asking his mother to hurry. She was surprised by this haste in a son who usually didn't like to go to the market. All the way, Osama was asking himself, "Will I see her again today?"

His mind kept busy all day long, thinking about the little girl's secret. He waited for her by the shore of the river, looking from time to time for any sign of her. But the place remained quiet, and she never showed up. Over the next several days, he repeated the same series of actions until he became desperate. He even started to ask himself if he'd imagined seeing her, and if maybe there was no girl at all. This was what he asked himself as he held a few pebbles, giving each a forceful toss so that they'd jump across the surface of the water before sinking down to the riverbed.

One day, he was sitting at the edge of the river, playing his favorite rock-skipping game. But when he turned to get another pebble, he saw a shadow behind one of the trees. He knew someone was watching him. "Who's there?" he shouted.

The shadow vanished suddenly among the trees, but not before Osama had glimpsed a white dress through the vines, and had heard the sound of broken leaves beneath running feet. "Don't run away from me again," he called out, louder. "I've been looking for you for a long time now... Please!"

The sounds stopped in the wake of his imploring call. He walked closer and saw her standing there among the trees, looking down at the ground with a blush. "What's your name?" Osama asked.

She paused a while before answering. "Reem."

"Mine's Osama." He smiled as he replied and sat on the ground. "Have you been living here lately?" he asked in a friendly tone. "Because I haven't seen you around before this."

His friendly tone melted away some of her blush. She nodded as she sat down beside him, leaning her back against a tree.

"Who do you live with?" he asked.

She paused a little before she answered. "Grandma." Her voice was as clear as flowing water, as lovely as the soft blue of her eyes. Yet he felt a lurking sadness in her voice, trying to emerge despite her efforts to suppress it.

He thought for a while. "I didn't know anyone lived back here. I don't even know what's out beyond those bushes."

"I came to live here after ... my parents died."

She said the last words with tears glittering in her eyes. He blamed himself and felt guilty for questioning her and bringing back those memories.

"I'm sorry... I didn't know."

She wiped the tears with the sleeve of her dress and stayed silent, not uttering a single word. He sat there, observing her, until she looked out at the horizon and said: "I have to go back before my grandma misses me."

"Wait!" He grabbed her hand as she was standing up. "Can I see you again?"

He let go of her hand when he noticed her timidity.

"I don't know," she said as she ran away, trying to hide her blush. "Maybe!"

Osama went back home, feeling a thrill of joy. His mother was puzzled by the sudden change in his mood, which was so different from the day before. She knew her son well, and she realized he must be keeping a secret. He didn't answer when she asked him why his mood had changed so drastically, and she decided not to argue or pressure him.

That night, he could scarcely fall asleep. He wondered

if he would see the girl again or not. He didn't know the reason behind his intense yearning to see her again. Something mysterious had touched his heart, and her image occupied his mind until he fell into a deep sleep. He woke the next morning and told his mother that he would go to the market ahead of her, which only added to her puzzlement. Among the trees, on the bank of the river, Osama sat and wondered: *Will I see her today?*

Something in his heart told him that he would, and his instinct was right, for Reem emerged like the morning sun, smiling and looking at him. He sprang to his feet. "I *knew* I'd see you today," he said.

"And how did you know?" She smiled.

"Just a feeling," he said, jabbing a finger toward his heart.

It wasn't long before an intimate friendship grew up between the two children, for they were both alone and without friends, and they both felt the need for each other. Osama felt that she resembled him, as she was alone like him. And once he'd learned of her parents' deaths, he'd felt an inexplicable fatherly kindness toward her, as if fate had put him in her path to become responsible for her. He began to tell her about his school, his mother, and his life, while she looked at him, smiling and listening. She didn't say much. Finally, after he felt that he'd said everything, he urged her to talk. So she began to think, and then she told him that she'd seen him many days before he saw her. Ever since she'd come to her grandmother's house, she'd grown used to wandering around the house and discovering its surroundings, and she was now comfortable in the natural world. Gradually, she began to wander further from home, until she saw him near the river, stirring her curiosity. For a while, she'd looked at him from a distance, but she didn't have the courage to speak to him until she stumbled on him by coincidence, and the rest is history.

"It's definitely the best coincidence in the world," Osama said, laughing.

In that way, Osama and Reem started to meet every day, to talk and invent simple games together, as well as to tell each other their secret thoughts. Gradually their friendship deepened, and every day when Osama returned home, he would long for just one thing, and that was the moment when he'd go back to the riverbank where he'd see Reem.

One day, Osama sat for longer than usual while waiting for Reem. She was a little late, but eventually she showed up. Yet when she did, he felt she was different from before. "What's the matter?" he asked.

She paused a little then smiled and shook her head. "Nothing."

He urged her to speak, but she said no more. He didn't want to burden her with his insistence, and it was a while before either of them said anything. Suddenly, she announced that she was leaving, and he was surprised by her early departure.

"Wait," he said, but she didn't wait, and instead hurried away. Her behavior confused him, and he decided that the next day, he had to ask her about what had happened. She was making him worried.

The next day, he sat waiting for her as usual. A long time passed without her showing up, and he stayed there waiting for her, without leaving his spot, until the evening grew dark and his mother came searching for him. She saw him sitting there in silence, and she felt very worried about him. "What's the matter, son?" she asked.

He shook his head. "Nothing."

This was the first time since Osama had met Reem that a day had passed without him seeing her, and this made him upset. Then a few days passed without any sight of her, and he grew depressed thinking about what could have happened to her. One day, while he was sitting by the river, throwing little rocks in carelessly as he tried not to think, suddenly he heard little footsteps behind him. He turned quickly to see Reem walking toward him. He sprung to his feet, rubbing his eyes in disbelief, then walked swiftly toward her. He almost hugged her, but he pulled himself together. "Where have you been these last few days?" he asked, as if blaming her.

"Don't worry," she said miserably. "It's my own problem."

"We're friends, and friends share everything, even their worries and their problems."

She couldn't help but smile at those mature words, out of step with his age, but she didn't answer and kept mysteriously silent.

"Next time you disappear I'll go looking for you," he said stubbornly.

"Please don't do that!" she said, fearful. "If one of these days you don't see me, don't come looking."

"Why do you say that?" He felt bewildered.

She looked into his eyes with a determination that jarred against her childish features. "Promise me!" she said.

In the face of her determination, he felt even more puzzled. "I promise."

And so they never returned to the topic of those days when Reem was absent. However, from that day, he felt her change. When she was sitting with him, she'd be anxious and nervous, glancing over her shoulder, as if looking for something. She also stopped spending as much time with him as she had before. This made Osama sad, and sometimes depressed, because he wanted to understand, to know what had happened with her! But the case remained as it was: a mystery.

Things went on in this way until he felt that they'd started to return to how they'd been before. He felt relieved by this, and he never spoke about her absence. With time, she started to regain her smile and shine. She no longer seemed anxious all the time.

Then, one day, Reem didn't show up. He waited for her for a long time, but there was no sign of her. She didn't show up the next day either, and he felt terribly worried. Would she come back again after an absence of many days, as she had the last time? He waited every day, but in vain. He thought about looking for her. He remembered his promise, but his worrying about her overcame his wish to keep it. He had to check on her.

His feet took him to the tangled bushes, and he forced his way through them. He'd never made it this far before, and he wasn't even sure he was taking the right path. Still, he let his heart lead him in his search for Reem. After a while, he felt a terror of the wild trees, although in his heart he knew she couldn't be very far. He'd met with her every day, so she *must* be near. With time, the thickness of the trees began to diminish, and his steps quickened until he reached a wide clearing in the woods, in the midst of which there was an old wooden house. In front of the house sat Reem, with a deep sadness in her eyes. She didn't notice his presence until he came close and shouted her name: "Reem!"

She looked at him in surprise, and then her expression turned to anger. "What are you doing here? Why did you come?" He was surprised by her reaction, but she continued angrily, "You promised!"

Before he could answer, he heard a loud hissing, and a black cat jumped down from the roof of the house, landing near him and trying to swipe at his face. He retreated in fear, and Reem rushed to hold back the cat. "Please, go, and never come back!" she begged him.

He had been terrified by the cat. He was also surprised by Reem's words, which set off reverberations of painful shock in his heart. He retreated with confused steps, looking at her once more before he ran back home.

The next few days, Osama snuck up close to her house, staying there among the trees and watching her sit there in silence, her eyes glittering with tears. As she did, the black cat sat close by, watching her with its unblinking eyes. Osama was sitting far enough away that she didn't notice his presence. He would be filled with sorrow and confusion, and then finally, after he felt she was safe, he would walk away. Until the day came when she didn't show up even there. He waited for her appearance all day, until it was dark. Then he saw a light in the window of the house. Now he knew for sure that someone was inside. He thought about knocking on the door to ask about her, but he didn't dare. And so the days passed without any sight of her until he grew desperate... What secret surrounds you, Reem. What secret?

4

THE CABIN AMONG THE TREES

Saif listened to Osama's story, astonished and bewildered. It felt as though every time he tried to solve the mystery, he found himself mired in more mysteries and secrets. "This is the weirdest thing I've ever heard in my life!" he said, once Osama had finished his story.

Osama nodded. He understood. "But it's all true, I swear."

"Where is this house where Reem and her grandmother live?" Saif asked.

"She lives there." Osama pointed toward the other side of the river. "If you cross the bridge and walk that way, you'll find a thicket of trees. Once you cross it, you'll find a clearing, and in the middle of all that is the old house."

Saif looked in the direction Osama was pointing. "Seems like I need to check it out myself to figure everything out."

"Can I come with you?" Osama asked eagerly.

Saif shook his head. "Better if I go alone."

Disappointment and anxiety spread across the young boy's face, so Saif patted his shoulder. "Don't worry, everything will be fine."

He waved goodbye to Osama and walked along the path he'd pointed out, crossing the small wooden bridge to the other side of the river. The cat followed him with its endless mewing, but he ignored it as he walked across the green grassy turf. At first, the trees were scattered here and there, but as time passed, he felt the trees grow thicker, until he reached brush so dense and tangled it blocked the sunlight and cast heavy shadows everywhere.

He stopped in front of an old wooden house, which stood alone among the trees. He approached it slowly, examining it as he did. There was nothing strange except for the old, unfamiliar architectural style—but nothing extraordinary. He took a deep breath to sort himself out before he knocked at the wooden door. He waited several moments, but there was no answer. He knocked on the door a few more times. There was no answer except for a complete silence.

After coming this far, Saif was not ready to turn back. He knocked more forcefully on the door, and the door—it wasn't tightly shut—opened from the impact of his pounding. He was afraid someone might think he was trying to break into the house, but he thought, *If after all that knocking, no one answered, then the house must be empty.*

He suspected it might not be the same house that the boy had been talking about. "Or maybe it's abandoned," he said, looking around at the coating of age that clung to the house. He hesitated a little as he stared at the open door. If anyone was inside, it wasn't right to enter without the owners' permission—but his curiosity was stronger than his hesitation. He stepped inside the house, preceded by his curious gaze, which examined everything. The house didn't look much different from the inside than it had outside. It was old—messy and dusty—and much of the furniture was concealed beneath by half-torn covers. The rest of the place didn't look any better than.

Saif might have decided the house was indeed abandoned if he hadn't seen a small stove and table. On the table was a plate, covered with crumbs, and a cup of tea with nothing left but the leaves. He raised the cup to his nose and sniffed cautiously. "Seems recent," he said.

He returned the cup to its place, now afraid, since he was certain the house was not abandoned. If anyone saw him now, they would think he was an intruder or a thief. He thought about slipping out of the house before he got into trouble. Suddenly he heard a faint moan that made him freeze as he looked around for the source of the sound. In front of him was a narrow corridor. He walked toward it, his ears fixed on following the faint sound. It seemed to come from behind a wooden door to his right. Saif turned the knob to open the door and walked into a small room that was just as careworn and neglected as the rest of the house. But in the middle of the room, there was a small bed. He approached it slowly and found a little blonde girl lying there.

Saif studied her: her skin was pale, her body was skinny, and her face was so thin that her cheekbones jutted out. She moaned, her eyes still closed, and it seemed she hadn't noticed him. He didn't know that to do, as everything about this was unnerving. *Is this the girl I'm looking for?* he asked himself.

He reached out steadily to touch the child's forehead and check on her. The moment his cold finger touched the girl's forehead, she opened her eyes and screamed in terror. He stumbled back in a panic toward the door. Suddenly he heard footsteps, felt a hand clutching his shoulder, and found himself staring into the face of an old woman. Her eyes burned with anger, and she seized him with a force that did not fit with her age or figure. "What are you doing in my house, you vile thief?" she asked fiercely.

At that moment, the cat jumped in front of them, mewling loudly. The old woman released his shoulder and took a step back. "What on earth is this?" she said in a surprised tone.

She shifted her gaze between Saif and the cat. "Now I see what's going on here…it seems," she muttered.

Saif rubbed his aching shoulder. "Well, *I* don't understand anything at all."

The young girl looked around her in fear. The old woman approached her and patted her shoulder. "Don't be afraid, my little one." Then she said with a strange tenderness, "You should take your medicine now."

The old woman took a glass vial from her pocket. Inside was a blood-red liquid. The little girl took several sips, then laid her head back against the pillow and closed her eyes. Saif wasn't sure whether she'd fallen asleep or was just pretending to sleep, but he felt pity for her evident weakness. He turned to the old woman, hoping to hear an explanation of what was happening. But when he opened his lips to speak, the old woman put a finger to her lips in a gesture of silence. Then she bundled up the cat in her arms—the creature was calm, as though it were used to this—and gestured to Saif to follow her.

He followed with quiet steps so as not to disturb the

sleeping girl. Once they were both outside the room, the old woman quietly closed the door and headed toward the house's front entrance. She sat on one of the chairs that stood around the small table and gestured to Saif to sit on the other. He sat down, feeling tense, and he didn't know what to say. "I apologize for breaking in," he mumbled. "I'm really not a thief."

The old woman smiled with understanding. "I realize that now," she said as she stroked the cat's fur. "When I saw the broken door, at first I thought it was a thief, and feared most for my little granddaughter, who can't defend herself. But when I saw my cat with you, I figured it out."

Saif was confused, and his thoughts grew tangled, which was obvious from his incoherent sentences. "Your cat? I don't understand! I bought this cat from a pet store... then it acted strange... it made me lose my temper... and I found myself...here..."

The old woman's smile didn't change, nor did the repetitive movement of her hand on the cat's back. "It's all right," she said. "I understand what happened."

"I also want to understand!"

She gave a heavy sigh. "It's complicated, and I don't know how to explain it to you."

They both sat in silence for a few moments, before she put the cat aside and stood up. She filled the teakettle with water and lit the stove's single burner.

"As I just told you," she said. "I own this cat."

"I understood that," he said impatiently. "But I have a lot of other questions."

She sat once again, stroking the relaxed cat between her arms. "A long time ago, I was living alone with my daughter," she said. "She was the only thing I had in this world. I spared no effort in raising her, and I did everything a mother could do in this world. But the poor thing… I don't know what I did wrong in raising her."

Saif didn't understand what all this had to do with the subject at hand, but her words aroused his interest. "What happened to your daughter?"

The old woman sighed and went on. "When my daughter grew into a teenager, she fell in love with a young man of these times. Well, you know what I mean, these reckless wealthy types."

He nodded, even though she didn't pay him any attention. She went on talking as if she were recalling a distant memory. "This young man wanted her, and he proposed more than once, but I rejected him for obvious reasons. Yet my disrespectful daughter decided to run away with him, and marry him far away from me, and I never heard news of her again…or not for a long time."

At those final words, her eyes glittered with tears, and she sighed passionately. "After nearly two years of marriage, she sent me a letter telling me that she'd given birth to her first child, a beautiful girl, and that I was now a grandmother. My heart had softened toward her, and I wished that she'd come back. But I never saw her again."

The last words caught in the old woman's throat, and tears flowed from her eyes.

"What happened?" Saif asked.

The old woman paused a moment. "My daughter and her husband died in a car accident."

At that moment, the whistling of the kettle burst out, coinciding with her last words, startling Saif. The old woman got up and turned off the flame, then prepared two cups. "How many sugars?" she asked Saif.

"Just one, please."

She added the sugar and tea, poured in the boiled

water, and stirred the mixture. Meanwhile, Saif was thinking about her words, and he was eager to know more. She put the teacup in front of him and returned to her chair.

"It was several years after the girl's birth," she said. "It was the sort of car accident that might happen to anyone, but by the will of God the girl survived. After the authorities made sure I was her relative, one of the lawyers brought the young girl to live with me. I told myself that God had compensated me for the loss of my daughter, who'd run away and left me while still a teen."

As he listened, Saif sipped from his cup. He remembered then that he hadn't eaten his breakfast. The air was still chilly, which made the cup of tea even more welcome. A sweet numbness ran through his body as he went on listening to the old woman's tale.

"But it seems this naughty little girl has inherited the stubbornness of her mother." Some sharpness snuck into the old woman's voice. "A little while after she'd arrived, I noticed that she would leave the house and spend a lot of time outside. I ordered her not to go outside, and not to go far from the house. Even so, she disobeyed me, and she kept on leaving the house without my knowledge, spending a long time outside. Then I discovered, by coincidence, that she had befriended one of those brats. I saw how much she was like her mother, and I was afraid it would be a repetition of the same fate."

Saif sipped the last of the tea and put the cup aside. "It's a touching story, and I feel sorry for your daughter," he said. "But what has this story got to do with the *cat*?"

"The cat?" the old woman muttered as she looked at the teacup. "Yes, have I told you that it's my cat? It's actually my servant."

Saif didn't understand her final words, and felt a haziness blurring his mind. "Excuse me?"

At this moment, the cloudiness seized his consciousness. His mind fell into a deep darkness, and he collapsed at the feet of the old woman.

5

INTO THE UNKNOWN

Young Reem could not have imagined the extent to which her life would turn upside down after the deaths of her parents in the accident. The concept of death seems distant—even unimaginable—to the mind of a child, until that child loses someone close to their heart. Then they begin to realize the cruelty of death, and what it means when someone who was once so close ceases to exist. For Reem, it wasn't just anyone. These were the two closest people in her life. Perhaps they were the only ones close to her; she had no friends at her age, no relatives who came to visit, and no relatives they visited. At first, she didn't understand why, but eventually she realized that her parents' marriage had happened without permission from both families, because of differences in social class and other vague reasons she failed to grasp. And so she lived, knowing nothing about her relatives.

After the incident, Reem found herself alone, confused, and torn apart. Relatives on her father's side refused to accept her into their homes. They said that she belonged to her mother, and so they searched for her only living relative from her mother's side: her grandmother.

Reem had never heard her mother talk much about her grandmother, and sometimes she felt that her mother was trying to escape from her childhood memories. Shadows of sorrow hung over her eyes whenever they talked about it, so Reem ignored the subject and stopped asking too much about her grandmother. Then, when she found herself on her way to live with her, she felt a sense of awe and a fear of the unknown. That day, she sat in a car beside the lawyer, who drove her up to her grandmother's after he'd told her everything. He was a friend of her father's, and he'd looked after her until the matter was settled. At last, when they reached the outskirts of the small town where her grandmother lived, they found her waiting for them. When she saw the child, she hugged her, which eased part of Reem's fear. The lawyer told her that he'd done his job, and he bid farewell to the both of them.

As she walked next to her grandmother, heading towards her new home, Reem felt a confused mix of emotions. She was about to be introduced to a new and unfamiliar life. On the way, she looked at her grandmother, who had still not exchanged a single word with her, but who held her hand tightly as she walked beside her. She suddenly found herself in a quiet wooded district. For Reem, who had spent her whole life in the crowded city, the place became even more awe-inspiring. Her grandmother approached a small wooden house among the trees. Then she opened the door and welcomed Reem into her new home.

She did not like the look of the house, as neglect emerged from every part of it. But she excused her grandmother, since she'd lived alone. Still, Reem wasn't comfortable knowing that she had to live in this place. Her grandmother let her wander around in the house, and Reem screamed in horror when a black cat suddenly jumped in front of her, hissing angrily.

Her grandmother walked up and hurried to hold the cat. "Don't be afraid, my girl," she said. "This is the companion that comforts me in my loneliness. It won't hurt you."

Reem didn't like the cat's strange and frightening appearance. She didn't know why her grandmother would keep an animal like that in her home. She told herself that old age could make people do strange things, but she realized from the first moment—for some unclear reason—that she didn't like this cat, and that she didn't want it anywhere near her. Yet at first she said nothing about it to her grandmother. She didn't want to be a nuisance.

Reem's first days at her grandmother's house were long and boring. Her grandmother left the house every day, leaving her all alone, and Reem neither knew where her grandmother was going nor when she would come back. She felt strange sitting at home, all alone, crying whenever she remembered her parents. She didn't think about leaving the house because she didn't know the area and feared she would lose her way. And her grandmother didn't seem interested in taking her along with her. Despite her desire to be with her grandmother, she felt relieved whenever her grandmother left the house, because she took the black cat with her, which removed the burden of fear from Reem's chest ever so slightly.

One day, while Reem was alone in the house, she felt constricted, as if the air in the stuffy house was choking her. So she overcame her fears and hesitations, and she decided to go out for a walk. At first, she was frightened, as the house was so isolated, and there were no other houses nearby. But she enjoyed the view of the surrounding trees. After she got used to wandering around, the love of nature began to sneak into her heart. Every day, as soon as her grandmother left the house, she would go out to walk among the trees and breathe in the fresh cold morning air. Eventually, her feet took her to the river near the house. She liked to sit near the bank, glancing over at the sight of the various reflections that played on the sheet of water. Yet not once did she dare to cross it and go to the other side. She began to believe that this was her own world, and her imagination filled the place with life.

On one of her usual walks, Reem glimpsed a boy she'd never seen before, sitting near the river. He seemed to be about the same age as her. She watched him from afar without making a sound; she didn't have the courage to approach and talk to him. This went on for the next few days, and every time she would watch him from afar in her usual silence, and this—somehow—eased her loneliness. Until one day, when she was walking, distracted by her own thoughts, and unaware of her surroundings, she found herself in front of the young boy. She felt hot blood rushing to her cheeks, and she didn't know what to do except run away from him. Later, she didn't understand why she'd done it, except that shyness had spurred to run. That evening, after she'd had dinner with her grandmother, she sat in her bed, staring at the moonlight that snuck through the tree branches and in through her window, thinking about the boy. She thought that she must certainly have frightened him, and she blamed herself.

The next morning, she hesitated a bit, wondering if she should go to the same place or not. Her shyness stopped her from going there, so instead she wandered around near the house. Until one day, when she decided to go and watch him from afar, as she'd done before. *It has been several days since we met. He might not even be going there any more.*

The idea that she might not see him again made her feel gloomy. Although she'd never talked to him, she felt he was her only company. So she made up her mind and went to where she used to see him, half-expecting that he wouldn't be there. But there he was, sitting and looking sad as he cast a few small stones into the river. She went on watching him, silently, until he turned his face and saw her. She tried to run again, but he called to her, so she stopped, and he tried to speak with her. They exchanged a few words. She learned his name, and she told him hers. She didn't want to talk much about herself, but she felt comfortable in those minutes she spent with him.

A few days passed, and Osama became a part of her day. She grew used to his presence in her life, and he was her consolation in all those difficult days. One day, she went home to find her grandmother waiting for her, her grandmother's features twisted up in an expression of anger. Reem, frightened, spoke first. "Hi, Grandma!"

Her grandmother ignored her greeting. "Where have you been?"

"I was walking around the house to get to know the place."

Her grandmother stared into her eyes. "Since when do you go outside without telling me?"

Reem was puzzled by her grandmother's anger. "I didn't do anything wrong!"

"And what were you doing?"

"I didn't do anything." She avoided her grandmother's direct gaze. "I was just walking around to breathe in some fresh air."

Her grandmother looked at her doubtfully. "Just don't go out without telling me. I was worried about you."

Reem nodded without saying a word, and then went to her room. At lunch, she didn't exchange a single word with her grandmother. She decided that she'd tell Osama about what had happened with her grandmother when they met the next day, to ask what he thought she should do.

The next morning, she waited until her grandmother went out as usual with the cat. Then she walked toward the place where she met Osama. On the way, she thought about what she would say to him. Once she saw him on the horizon, sitting on the riverbank, her heart beat faster and faster as she moved swiftly towards him, and he welcomed her with joy. She'd thought about what she could say to him, but now no words came to mind; she didn't want to worry him. She spent some time with him before she told him she had to go home. Then, abruptly, she left. As she was walking among the trees, she felt a hand grip her tightly. She turned in panic to find her grandmother giving her a cold stare that froze the very blood in her veins.

"So this is the one you leave the house to meet."

She clasped Reem's hand and dragged her all the way back home. Fear sealed Reem's lips, such that she didn't speak all the way. Once they got home, her grandmother shouted: "From this day on you will never leave the house. I will not allow the same mistake that happened with your mother to be repeated with you."

Reem didn't understand what her mother had to do with all of this. Her only concern was to defend herself. "I didn't do anything wrong!" Anger began to replace her fear.

"Yes, you did, you lied to me!" Her grandmother turned her angry gaze toward her. "For this wretched boy!"

Reem didn't understand the reason behind her grandmother's anger. She felt there must be some secret cause for all this rage.

"If I find out that you're going out to meet this brat, your punishment will not be a light one!" Her grandmother fumed. "Nor will he be safe from that punishment, do you understand?"

Reem's grandmother looked terrifying as she uttered these words. Reem could not respond; in fear, she dashed off toward her room, threw herself on her bed, and loudly wept. She stayed in her room the whole day, scarcely moving until she fell asleep. The next day, she didn't exchange a word with her grandmother. She began to grow afraid and no longer felt comfortable at home. "Don't leave the house while I'm outside," her grandmother said with an exacting glare. "Am I clear?"

Reem mumbled something and turned her face away. Her grandmother kept on staring at her for a while, and then she left the house, leaving her alone. Reem decided to stay at home, since she feared her grandmother's anger. She knew that Osama would be worried about her, but she didn't dare disobey her grandmother's orders by going out to meet him. As hard as it was, the day eventually passed. And so passed the many days that came after it, until Reem finally decided to sneak out, meet Osama, and return before her grandmother knew it.

She managed to go and see him, but she didn't tell

him anything. Her anxiety stopped her from being open with him as she always had been before. Her mind was churning with fear at the thought that her grandmother might find out that she'd left the house. But several days passed without any problem. Until, one day, she came back home to find her grandmother waiting for her with fury in her eyes. Reem was horrified.

"So. You dared to violate my orders!"

Reem's heart was in her mouth. "What do you want from me?"

"I want you to carry on our legacy." Her grandmother approached her. "The legacy your mother ran from, when she went off to marry that rich young fop. The legacy I fear you will try to run from as well. Our lineage must not end."

From between her tears, Reem looked up at her grandmother in puzzlement. She didn't utter a word.

"You're too young to understand," her grandmother said, after she'd calmed down. "There's a long road ahead, and there are many things we must do to prepare you to be worthy to carry on our great legacy. Everything I do is for you, and so it angers me that you might spoil everything with your childish folly."

Then Reem's grandmother walked up and grabbed Reem shoulders, apparently deciding to be honest. "I know my daughter didn't tell you anything about your origins. But you, my child, are no ordinary girl, and so it was with your mother. We come from a long line of *witches*, and this has been passed down for generations. Every witch must pass on her magic to her children. But my daughter refused to bear this great legacy, and she escaped to marry that foolish young man. But fate has compensated me. You are the one who will inherit my gifts."

"You're lying! I don't believe you!" Reem shook her head in denial, tears running down her cheeks. "My mother was not a witch!"

"Your mother was not, because your mother was a coward and ran away. However, you will become a witch. This is what I will do for you, and you should be grateful for it."

Reem was in shock, her mouth clamped shut. Her grandmother didn't seem to be joking. She'd always felt that her mother was afraid of her grandmother, which was why she didn't like to talk about her. Now, Reem started to understand why. Her grandmother either really was a witch, or she was a crazy old woman, and both possibilities were equally scary. Reem rushed to her room in fear, jumped in her bed, and wrapped herself up in her blanket. She sobbed, wishing that this was all a nightmare, and that she was going to wake up.

That evening, as Reem lay in bed, swinging between wakefulness and sleep, she heard strange sounds coming from the hall. She quietly slipped out of her bed and stepped out of her room. She found her grandmother sitting in the center of a circle of candles that cast a frightening shadow over her face. Before her, the black cat lay on the ground as she stroked its body. An inscrutable chanting echoed from her mouth. The enigmatic scene terrified her so much that she retreated to her room before her grandmother could notice her. She shuddered under her blanket until she fell asleep.

The next morning, she opened her eyes and remembered the weird dream she'd had about her grandmother. These thoughts were interrupted by the meowing of the black cat, which was in the room, staring at her with its cold eyes. She screamed out in panic, but the cat did not seem to be affected by the loud noise. She rushed out of the room and was followed by the cat's agile steps. She looked for her grandmother and found her sitting in her wooden chair, drinking a cup of hot tea.

"What was the cat doing in my room?" Reem asked.

Her grandmother took a few more sips from her cup. "From now on, the cat will watch over you," she said. "He won't take his eyes off you. That way, I'll make sure you will never do anything behind my back again."

Reem stared at her in disbelief. But after her grandmother left the house, the cat began behaving strangely—it walked right behind her, following her everywhere. So she decided to get rid of it before her grandmother came back. She tried by many different means: to drive it out, to hit it, to carry it away from home and leave it alone. But it came back every time. Her grandmother had done something to this cat, something not natural! She remembered the dreadful nightmare she'd had the night before, and realized that it hadn't been as she'd thought, that it hadn't been a nightmare! There was now no doubt her grandmother had extraordinary powers, and this made Reem feel lonelier than ever. In the days that followed, she didn't try to meet Osama even once. She was afraid that her grandmother might hurt him, so she spent her time at home, or near it, sitting there, sunk in her thoughts, immersed in her sorrows. One day, she heard his voice calling out her name, and then she saw him in front of her. She was startled, and a mix of different emotions struck her heart—she was torn between longing for him, fear for him, and anger at him because he hadn't kept his promise. She told him to go back, that she could no longer see him.

In this way, the days passed for Reem, bleak and gloomy. She no longer spoke or did anything but sit in silence. She thought about running away, but how would she do it, and where would she go? She told herself that, if she wanted to escape, she must first get rid of the black cat. The idea filled her with enthusiasm, and it gave her a reason to do something other than sit there being depressed. There was a wooden bookshelf in the hall, and the books on it seemed to be organized, unlike the rest of the messy house. Reem had not approached the books before, but now she thought that she'd look at them while her grandmother was outside. To the cat's eyes, what she was doing wasn't peculiar, so it stretched its front legs and lay down before her. As it did, she sat on the floor, holding an old book that she'd pulled off the wooden shelf. The pages were yellowed with age, and they were full of bizarre symbols and uncanny drawings, and she couldn't make any sense of them. Then she realized that these books belonged to the art of witchcraft. They were spells, potions, and other strange things. She no longer had any doubt that her grandmother was indeed a witch. What she read had aroused her curiosity, and, at the same time, it also increased her fear. Reem's grandmother belonged to another world that was alien to her. She wished she could go back to her past, to her ordinary life with her parents, but that seemed like a distant dream.

As the days passed, she read more of these books, motivated by her curiosity, passion, and a desire to know more. Sometimes, she would hide a book in her room without her grandmother's knowledge, to read in the evening, closing the door to her room and shutting herself inside. Reem became fascinated by this strange world, feeling a mixture of astonishment and fear. In the days that came, she was absorbed by those extraordinary arts. Until, one day, she discovered a very intriguing thing: a book hidden in a secret drawer of her grandmother's bookshelf. She found it by chance, as she was hunting among the books. It was an old tome, with an illustration of an ugly black cat and a hideous skull on its cover. The cover both terrified and intrigued her. She hoped this book had something to do with her grandmother's black cat, and she hid the book beneath her bed until evening. When she was sure that her grandmother had fallen into a deep sleep, she took the book from underneath her bed and lit a candle so she could see its pages. She threw herself into reading this book, and she devoured its characters. The book was about the servants of witches, usually a black cat, and the various kinds of enchantments and magics that a witch could practice on it. Finally, Reem understood the charm her grandmother had cast on the black cat, a kind of magic called the Tracking Spell. Through it, a witch could make her cat watch someone without ever turning aside from their task. Eagerly, Reem looked for a way to get rid of the charm. She found that the only way to get rid of it was for someone to acquire this cat *willingly*.

That night, Reem could not sleep. When she realized there was some way of escaping the cat's steely gaze, and running away from her grandmother, she was filled with excitement. But what would she do next? She loved the idea of living with Osama, and she wished it could be possible—it seemed to her a beautiful dream, and it would be so beautiful if it could come true.

The next morning, Reem waited until her

grandmother left the house as usual. After that, she waited for a while to make sure her grandmother was far away from home. Then she, in her turn, picked up the cat and left. She didn't know where her feet were leading her. She got to the river where she used to meet Osama, but he wasn't there. She didn't know if that upset or relieved her. She didn't want to involve him in her troubles. So, for the first time, she stepped on the small wooden bridge and crossed the river. She had never gone so far from her grandmother's house, and she was afraid. Soon, she found herself in the middle of the crowded market that lay on the other side of the river. She didn't know where she was going; all she could think about was getting as far from home as possible and getting rid of that cat. But how could she convince someone to take it willingly? She blamed herself for not having a plan before she'd left the house. She'd been so focused on the idea of running away that this obvious point hadn't even occurred to her. She couldn't just walk up to a stranger and ask, *Hey, would you like to have this wonderful cat?* The very idea of it was ridiculous. She thought about all the possibilities as she walked, adrift in the city streets.

Suddenly it occurred to her that she might sell it to a pet store. In that way, someone might take it willingly, and she would get rid of it. She liked the idea, but as she looked at the ugly black cat, she doubted that anyone would want to buy it—no matter how cheap the price. Still, she had to try. She asked for directions until she reached one of the nearby pet stores. After some negotiations with the shop owner, she managed to sell the cat cheaply. She left the shop feeling free at last. She had gotten rid of the cat.

Confused, Reem walked through the streets of the city,

unsure where to go. Should she look for Osama? But if she did, she was afraid he might get involved in something bigger than he could handle. She walked aimlessly, with no destination, without any expectation of what would happen next. Then she felt a hand grasp her tightly. She shouted in pain as she turned, searching for the face of whoever held her. Her eyes met those of her angry grandmother.

"Oh, you ungrateful child!"

"How did you find me?" Reem asked, in pain.

Her grandmother dragged Reem by the hand so that they were side by side. "I knew that you'd get rid of the cat, I predicted it," she said. "But I meant to get to you before you got rid of him. You're smarter than I expected. But that's a good sign, it means you'll be a clever witch and I'll be proud of you."

Despite her grandmother's rage, Reem refused to tell her where she'd left the cat. So her grandmother dragged her back toward the house. "I'll make sure that you never leave the house without my knowledge again."

Reem didn't answer. She remained silent as she walked, with unwilling steps, until they reached the house. The sight of it depressed her, and she ran to her room, where she threw herself onto the bed and burst out crying.

Reem stayed in her room, having no desire to step outside it. She wanted to be left alone, and her grandmother didn't try to talk to her until evening, when she called her to come eat. Reem ignored the call, but her grandmother repeated it many times, until Reem stood up heavily, walked toward the dining table, and sat in front of her grandmother. She began to eat the steaming-hot food.

She ate without any real appetite, and then noticed that her grandmother was sitting in silence, not eating with her. She guessed that her grandmother was still angry because of the cat, but she didn't care and went on eating alone. But she didn't just eat alone at that meal; it became her grandmother's habit not to eat with her. Reem didn't mind. She got used to eating alone. After a few days, Reem began to feel very weak. She couldn't leave her bed, and any movement required great effort. Her grandmother began to bring her food to the bed, and she prepared a medicine for her, saying it would cure her. Even though she didn't trust her grandmother, Reem couldn't oppose her. Her grandmother gave her the medicine, then she stroked Reem's hair and said in a peculiar tone, "Don't worry, my little one. Soon everything will be over."

6

IN THE WITCH'S CELLAR

Saif slowly regained consciousness. As he did, he felt a headache as if a thousand hammers were slamming into his head. The question *What's going on?* echoed in his mind. He opened his eyes to see where he was, trying to understand what was happening, but at first he could see nothing. He closed his eyes again, trying to remember what had happened. He remembered the cat, the girl named Reem, the old woman, and his conversation with her… But what brought him *here*? He closed his eyes and opened them several times before realizing that the place was pitch black. Was it night already! How long had he been in this place? He tried to move and realized that his hands and feet were tied to a bed. He panicked, flailing his hands in violent jerks in an attempt to free himself, but this only increased the pain in his wrists and ankles. His eyes started to grow used to the darkness, and, in the very dim light sneaking in from somewhere, he realized that he was being kept in a narrow, foul-smelling room, probably a cellar! Once he realized this, claustrophobia seized his mind, taking over.

"Is anyone here?" he shouted in terror. He heard no reply, so he repeated his call again and again. Every time, there was no answer save the deafening silence.

"Damn you!" he cried in anger.

He knew he needed to calm his nerves and pull himself together, so he lay back and closed his eyes. He worked to sharpen his other senses: it was completely quiet, and he could not hear anything. A foul odor surrounded him, and this only deepened his misery. Then he felt a light breath of air coming from somewhere.

He opened his eyes, searching for the source, and spotted a small opening from which faint moonlight had slipped in. The room seemed even narrower than before, and he had a hard time breathing.

Saif's thoughts were interrupted by the sound of a door opening. As it opened, light crept in, followed by a human figure carrying an old, fire-burning oil lantern. Saif could not see whether it was the old woman, but instinctually he knew. Then came her voice: "So you're finally awake."

By now, she'd come close enough for him to see her features. The air that came from the small opening made the flame of the oil lantern dance, casting frightening shadows on her face.

Saif broke out in a cold sweat. "What have you done to me?" he asked, his voice trembling. "Did you drug me?"

"Oh, I'm *sorry*," she said sarcastically. "It seems I haven't told you yet that I am a witch."

He didn't understand what she meant, but he felt the mockery in her tone. "I can't believe I was fooled by your false words and fake tears." His fury showed clearly on his features. "You really are an excellent actress."

As he spoke, he tried to find a way to free himself of

his bonds. He wondered what strength this old woman had to be able to bind him so tightly.

"It wasn't a lie, young man." She shook her head with a cold smile. "Actually, I've told you only half of the truth. Everything I said about my daughter is true. But the real reason she ran away from home was that she didn't want to carry on our family legacy. She refused to become a witch. She resisted her fate."

Then her voice filled with a bitter anger, as though she were recalling the most unpleasant of memories. "She preferred to run away and marry that rich young fop, rather than continue my legacy and become a magnificent witch like me. She wanted to shatter the family line, which has practiced witchcraft for tens of generations."

Then she clenched her right fist, waving in the air. "Then her daughter came, and I thought that this was my chance to make up for the loss of my own daughter. But I've found that she's just like her mother. She *refuses* to become a witch. But I know how to make her forget that brat, even if I had to get rid of him."

Saif was now certain that the old woman was unstable. Witch or no, she was very dangerous. He tried to hold himself together. "And what about me? What has any of this got to do with me?"

"You?" she asked, as if she were waking up from a long dream. "You have nothing to do with any of this." She regained her cold smile. "Believe me, I have no grudge against you at all. You're just an unfortunate stranger who got caught up in things that are beyond his understanding, greater than the tangible world he touches. There is a thin veil that blinds your eyes to the things that happen right under your nose, things you cannot glimpse. But everything will be revealed to you soon."

"Why don't you just let me go?" he asked, anxious.

"Leave?" She gave a malicious laugh, followed by a sharp smile. "You can't just walk away now that you know all this. *Maybe* I told you all this because I have no intention of letting you leave." She paused for a while, then added vaguely, "I'll need you in the final ritual, to turn my granddaughter into a witch."

Those last few words struck him hard. "What do you mean by 'the final ritual'?" he asked, still trying to unfasten his bound hands.

She thought a little. "No harm in telling you more to satisfy your natural human curiosity. Anyhow, you won't be able to leave this place, and you'll see it all with your own eyes."

The light in the lantern continued to flicker. "I've decided to turn my granddaughter into a witch, even if she does not want to be one of us, in order to preserve our great lineage." Frightening shadows moved across the old woman's face. "I gave her all those potions to prepare her for the change she'll undergo. But the final transformation requires a last sacrifice to the demons." Then she leaned over him and added in a hissing voice: "human sacrifice."

Her voice sent shivers down his spine. "But why *me*?" he asked in terror.

"I didn't choose you on purpose, as I told you. You are just a miserable unfortunate." She gave her shoulders a careless shrug. "I was planning to use that sticky brat my granddaughter calls Osama. However, on second thought, there's no doubt people will be concerned about his disappearance. But no one knows you came here, and your disappearance will not arouse any suspicions."

She turned, holding the lantern. "Don't worry, you won't have to wait long. Tomorrow, the full moon will be here, and by midnight, my granddaughter will be ready to become a witch. I will complete the ritual with a sacrifice."

She glanced back over her shoulder at him before she closed the door. "Enjoy the last day of your pathetic life."

She gave a final sarcastic laugh as she gave the door a great slam that echoed through the room, which sank, once again, into total darkness.

Saif wracked his brains, trying to think of a way to get himself out of this mess. He tried to unfasten his bonds, but he failed miserably. He was determined to escape this place at any cost. The old woman could either be insane or a real witch—either way, his life was in danger. He couldn't stay here. With his violent frightened movements, his hands and feet began to bleed, and the hot blood seeped onto everything. But his terrible panic blinkered his mind from the pain. He had no idea how much time had passed in this total darkness as he tried in vain to loosen the ties, until he completely lost hope. He surrendered again to his bonds and his despair. When he closed his eyes, the pain began to crawl into his mind.

Suddenly, he was startled by the sound of the door opening—this time, without the light from the oil lantern. Through the dim light that came from behind the door, Saif saw a figure entering the room. This person was shorter than the old woman. Then he heard the young girl's exhausted voice. "You're in danger. You have to escape."

This was the granddaughter of the old woman, the mysterious girl he'd been looking for all day. Here she was, right in front of him. She tried to unfasten the ties around his right hand. But it was bound too tightly, so she took a small knife out of her pocket and began to cut at the rope.

"Be careful with that thing," he said, watching with

concern. But by the time he finished speaking, the rope was severed. He took the knife from her, gripped it in his right hand, and sliced through the remaining ropes that bound his left hand and his feet. He was free at last, and he felt the joy of moving freely again.

"My knife, please." Reem opened her hand, palm up.

He hesitated. "This could be dangerous for a little girl."

She kept her palm open, looking at him without a word. He sighed and put the knife in her palm. "Fine. Anyway, you saved my life."

She put the knife back in her pocket, hiding it well. "I'm sorry, I didn't mean to get you involved in this." When she finally spoke, there was regret in her voice.

Saif felt pity for this girl, who bore a burden too heavy for her tender years. "Don't worry, it's not your fault. Lots of things happen to us in this world without our choosing. We give in to the flow—we let it drive us along—and we settle down where it casts us. You're the prey, not the predator, my young friend."

"But Grandma will force me to become a witch," she said, fear creeping into her voice. "I refused, but she made me drink this strange liquid, claiming it was medicine, except I feel much worse since I started taking her so-called medicines."

Then she added, in a horrified voice: "Then she told me about this dreadful ritual." Her eyes filled with tears, and her voice broke. "I don't want ... anyone to die ... because of me."

"Don't worry, no one will die." He sympathized with this child. "I won't let your grandmother hurt anyone."

When he mentioned Reem's grandmother, she looked

over her shoulder in fear. "She might come back at any time," she said. "You have to leave right now."

Saif didn't want to leave the little girl alone, but she begged him: "Please, run away!"

Reem led him up the stairs, where he found himself in the narrow corridor. He moved through it into the house's entryway, and then he opened the front door. Finally, he finally would get out of this cursed house! But then he found the black cat in front of him, arching its back and hissing angrily. Saif gave the cat a furious kick and ran away from the house as hard as he could.

Saif found himself crossing the small wooden bridge over the river, and running through the marketplace's darkened streets, which were silent as the grave, devoid of both vendors and customers. Nothing but the sound of the singing insects filled the night, and the far-off howling of a dog. Saif didn't meet any other human or living thing, save two cats fighting over some of the remnants of the market. But they jumped out of his way when they saw him running like the devil.

Saif saw light coming from the windows of the houses that appeared on the horizon. He thought, *There are people there, who are safe in their homes and have no idea about what is going on with me.* He envied those people and wished he were safe and warm at home right this minute. He kept running until he reached his car. It was waiting for him just where he'd left it that morning. He searched his pockets with shaky fingers, looking for the key, and he sighed in relief when he found it. With trembling hands, he opened the door and managed to turn on the engine. The wheels of the car gave a sharp squeal as he sped away. He couldn't believe that he'd finally escaped this hell.

Saif drove at an insane speed at this late hour, through roads that were empty of cars and passersby. From time to time, he'd pass through a traffic light flashing in dim yellow. The roar of the engine broke the silence of the night, and he drove on until he reached home. He hurried to park his car in the garage, then opened the front door to his house, locking it behind him with the key and the latch. Then he made sure to lock the back door as well, and he closed all the windows. He went to his bedroom and sat on the bed, knees pulled up against his chest. He pulled the covers over his shoulders, in shock about his last few hours. He found it hard to believe that all of it had really happened.

7

THE WITCHES' SHADOWS

Osama decided to carefully follow Saif; he couldn't let him go to Reem's house alone. Osama was very concerned about the man, and he also wanted to know what Saif would find in his search. Really, what he wanted was to make sure Reem was all right. He saw Saif knocking on the door until it opened, and then he saw him—hesitantly—enter the house. Osama sat near the house, waiting for what would happen next. A long time passed without Saif reappearing, which made Osama worry. He also knew that he himself was late, and that his mother would be worried, but he couldn't leave without checking on Reem and Saif. He thought about going into the house to see what was happening, but as he was thinking it over, he saw Reem's grandmother step out of the house and walk toward the thick, tangled trees. He couldn't make up his mind. Should he wait here for Saif, or should he follow the old woman? In the end, he decided to follow the old woman. Just seeing her aroused his curiosity.

So he followed her among a stand of trees he'd never

walked through before. The trees kept getting denser and denser, until he was barely able to see properly. Never before had he gone this far in. He felt his way around cautiously, and, at the same time, he was careful time to make sure the old woman didn't sense him sneaking up behind her. He was amazed to see her walk with such incredible confidence, and wondered how she knew her way among these trees? After a long walk, the old woman suddenly stopped, and Osama also came to a halt in his tracks, wondering why she'd stopped. Suddenly, in the midst of the dim light, he realized that she was not alone. She began to chant in a strange manner, words that he could not decipher. Out from the shadows of the thick forest, three other dark-faced elderly women appeared, wrinkled and ferocious-looking.

"Why did you summon us?" one of them asked, and he realized that she was talking to the grandmother.

"I've found a human sacrifice at last." And then she laughed in a thin voice that sent the shivers down Osama's spine. A monstrous delight was etched on the faces of the elderly women.

"The full moon's tomorrow," one of the women said. "Are you ready to live up to your side of the bargain?"

"Everything is ready," the grandmother said, nodding. "The sacrifice will be done on time."

The other witch congratulated her in advance for her granddaughter's transformation. Osama heard all this in disbelief. He wished that it was all a nightmare, but he knew it was all actually happening. He decided to flee before the old women noticed him. However, as he moved away to escape, he knocked into an old tree trunk that lay on the ground. He fell with a loud crash, drawing the witches' attention. He looked at them, terrified, as one of them hissed as she approached him: "Interloper."

At that moment, Osama felt his consciousness leaving him, and he slumped to the ground.

Saif spent the whole night in bed, vigilant and alert. Any sound that reached his ears startled him, as if the witch or her black cat could be breaking into his house at any moment. Sometimes, he daydreamed and saw shadows passing through his mind. The only thing that saved him from going completely mad was watching the sun rise once more the next morning.

He looked at his watch and found it was time to get to work, but he had no desire to go *anywhere*. He called in, pretending to be sick and asking if it was all right for him to miss a day. His exhausted voice, which reflected the vigil and fatigue of the night before, helped him be convincing. After that, he got out of bed and decided to have a quick hot shower to wash away the evidence of the previous night. Then he made himself a light breakfast, even though he had no real appetite and only nibbled at it. He tried to watch TV to occupy his mind and keep himself from his thoughts, but as he stared at the screen with half his mind, the other half went on thinking. Even when he tried to read a book, he felt that he was staring at blank white pages; he couldn't focus on anything. He wished his mind were itself a blank white page.

By evening, Saif was lying on the couch in front of the TV, unaware of what was playing on the screen. It was just comforting noise, to make him feel he was not alone. It was a local channel, and suddenly it cut to a news broadcast about a child from the city who'd gone missing. When he looked up at the child's picture, he found it was Osama, the boy who'd showed him the way to the old house. He straightened up and listened carefully to what the broadcaster was saying. The child had been missing since the previous day, when he hadn't returned home. His mother had told the police, and they immediately went out to search for him, but he'd left no trace. Anyone who found him was to go to the nearest police station... and so on.

Saif felt he was on the brink of madness. Had Osama followed him? Had he fallen into the hands of the witch? What if she hurt the boy? What about informing the police—would they believe his stories about a witch and a black cat? No doubt they would think him insane!

He remembered what the old woman had told him about the sacrifice that would take place at midnight, during the full moon. He couldn't sit idly by when a child's life was at stake. So he made a wild decision—he would go to the witch's house to check it out one more time. This did indeed feel like an insane act, but it felt better than just sitting there and surely going mad.

So he found himself taking the car out of the garage and driving through the night, once again alone. His heart was beating so fast it almost leapt out of his chest as he thought about what he was getting himself into. He was going back to the hornet's nest of his own free will. Many times, he thought about stopping and turning back, but his fear for the poor boy kept him on his way. Finally, he reached the bridge that crossed the river. He got out of his car and locked it. He decided to continue on foot, so that the sound of the car's engine wouldn't attract attention.

He walked toward the witch's house the same way he'd

walked before. It took a while, but he reached the old house. In the light of the full moon, it looked almost haunted. Saif was nervous, and thought about going back, but he couldn't, not after he'd come this far. He had to find a way to get into the house without anyone noticing. This time, using the front door was not an option.

He walked around the house, thinking about the opening. It felt as if he were trapped in the cellar all over again. Luckily, he found it, but it was so narrow he could barely fit through. He hesitated a little, because of his claustrophobia, but then he heard a loud scream break the silence of the night. His blood went cold, and then he shook with anger.

"Damn it!" he said as he pushed his body through the tight opening. He pushed his way into the cellar and stood there, still in the darkness, until his eyes got used to the moon's dim light, which entered the cellar through the small opening. Then he walked toward the door and examined it. It wasn't tightly locked, and, after a few pushes, it got loose and swung open. He climbed the wooden ladder with cautious steps, careful not to make a noise that would betray his presence. Then he walked down the narrow corridor. He heard a weird murmur and saw a strange, dancing light coming from the house's entrance. He realized it was candlelight; he peered in and saw the most bizarre scene he'd ever witnessed in his life.

The old woman was standing in the middle of the entryway, arms spread as she chanted mysterious words, the meaning of which he couldn't grasp. On the ground beneath her was a red pentagram with a candle on every one of its corners. The light from the candles was dancing, casting shadows that threw fear into Saif's heart. He saw the black cat—the creature had its back turned to him as it watched the old witch practice her dreadful rituals. But what terrified him the most was the sight of Reem and Osama tied to two wooden chairs. Osama was unconscious, his body covered in wounds. At that moment, Saif understood the source of the screams he'd heard, and he realized how the old woman had painted the *red* pentagram. Saif grew nauseous, but he controlled himself. He had to save these two from the mad witch.

Slowly, he walked toward Reem, who noticed him and looked toward him sharply. He gestured to her to keep quiet, and then he reached for the knife in her pocket. He remembered its place well. He cut the ropes that tied her as the witch went on with her mysterious chanting. She didn't notice Saif, but the black cat did, and it jumped toward him, meowing loudly. Then the old woman saw what was happening. She looked at him in anger as the cat raked him with its claws. But this time, Saif had a weapon. He stabbed the cat in the neck with the knife. It shrieked in pain, its blood splattering on everything in the room, even staining the red pentagram itself.

"NO!" the old witch cried in terror, and she leapt toward Saif to strike the hand that held the knife. The blade fell to the ground, and he cursed in pain. She looked sadly at the cat lying on the ground, drawing its last breath, and then she looked up at Saif with rage burning in her eyes. "You!" she cried. "You've spoiled everything! What vile wind tossed you in my path?"

She strode toward him, hands raised, and he backed up in fear until he felt the wall at his back. There was no escape. He looked at the old witch approaching him, mumbling strange words, and he felt he could neither move nor defend himself. Suddenly, the darkness began to spread around him, shrouding everything. He could no longer see the entrance, nor the house around him, nor Reem and Osama. He could see only the witch, her eyes burning with a red fire, the only thing that illuminated in this immense darkness. He tried to speak, or cry out, or run away, but he felt his body would no longer obey him. He heaved loud, ragged breaths as he struggled for air. It felt as though he were suffocating, his face going blue.

"You have to pay for what you've done!" The witch spoke in a deep, dreadful voice. "You had the chance to run for your life, but you came back, and so you walked to your own death."

Saif saw death approaching, and he gave himself up to his fate. But then the witch's eyes widened, and the red fire went out of them. The darkness that had been shrouding him began to clear, and the place went back to normal. He saw the old woman turning around in disbelief, turning her back to Saif. He saw Reem's knife. It had pierced the old woman's back, driven in all the way up to the hilt. The old woman took a few steps, trying to grasp at Reem, who backed up in fear. But then the old woman collapsed, falling onto her face, right in the middle of the pentagram.

"Why did you do *that*?" Saif asked.

"I didn't want her to hurt anyone," Reem said, looking at her hands, tears choking her voice. "She'd gone completely insane! What she did to you and Osama…I had to stop her!"

Reem covered her eyes with her hands. Saif walked up and hugged her warmly, with a parental tenderness. "Don't worry," he said sadly. "Everything will be all right."

Suddenly the red pentagram shimmered with a frightening light, and the sound of crazy laughter echoed through the house. Light shrouded Reem, and her hair blew as if she were in the heart of a storm. Saif clung to her, fearing for her life. Suddenly, the pentagram turned into spurts of flame, and Reem cried out in pain. Saif heard a deep, inhuman voice coming from the heart of the flame, as if it were coming from the heart of the universe, or from an alien world: "The sacrifice was made."

Then he felt an incredible power pull Reem from his hands. He tried to hold onto her, but he felt her vanish into the flames.

"I hope we meet again!" Reem called as she gave in to the force pulling at her. Then the flames vanished as suddenly as they had appeared. Once they'd gone, there was no trace of Reem, or of the grandmother's body, or even the black cat. Nor was there any evidence of blood or the red pentagram.

Saif stood, stunned by what had just happened. Then he noticed Osama, who was unconscious from the loss of blood. He untied him and carried him on his shoulders, walking away from this cursed house, until he reached the bridge where he'd left his car. He put Osama gingerly in the back seat. He drove the car with a confused and disordered mind, not knowing what to do! In the end, he decided to go to the nearest hospital, to have them check Osama and see if they could help him. When they saw the signs of torture on child's body, they called the police. They interrogated Saif, and he told them that he'd found Osama lying on the road. He mentioned nothing of the horror he had truly seen. When Osama woke up, he said that he couldn't remember anything after the moment of his disappearance. Thus the case was blamed on persons unknown, and it was quietly closed.

Months passed after that horrific episode. At first, Saif was devastated. He couldn't go back to work for several days. Then he realized that being alone wouldn't help him, and would only drive him crazy, so he drowned himself in more and more work. But he still couldn't stop thinking about Reem. She was there, in some other part of this world, but *where*? He kept wondering: *What had really happened to her?*

With time, it all slipped to the back of his mind, and it no longer occupied him as before. He went back to his normal life and his ordinary chores. One day, after he'd trimmed the lawn, he was sitting on a wooden chair reading the newspaper. Suddenly, he was startled by the mewing of a small cat. He looked over at the sound and found a black cat walking toward him. Before he could move a muscle, he felt the presence of another person. He turned to see a young girl in a white dress coming up slowly, smiling as she said: "I told you we'd meet again."

ABOUT THE AUTHOR

Ahmed Salah Al Mahdi is an Egyptian author, translator, and literary critic who specializes in fantasy, science fiction and children's literature. He has four published novels to date. His young-adult fantasy *Reem* and his post-apocalyptic science-fiction novel *Malaaz: The City of Resurrection* were both published by Alkanzy in Egypt. *The Black Winter*, a prequel to Malaaz, was published by Jordan's Amnah, and a fantasy novel *The Greek Papyrus: The Envoy of Morpheus* came out from Sama publishing house in Egypt. He has also published a children's picture book, *The Brave Rabbit*, with Asala Publishing in Lebanon, and many children's short stories in monthly magazines. He has translated a number of works, including Arthur Machen's "The Great God Pan," "The Wendigo" by Algernon Blackwood, and "Gods of Pegana" by Lord Dunsany. He also translates graphic novels and comic books for the Emirati publishing house Kalimat, including *Heart and Brain: An Awkward Yeti Collection* and *Adulthood is a Myth: A Sarah's Scribbles Collection*. He writes literary criticism for various publications, such as *ArabLit, Al Mayadeen, Noon Post,* and *Comics Gate.*

Online: ahmedmahdi.net

www.ingramcontent.com/pod-product-compliance
Lightning Source LLC
Chambersburg PA
CBHW071535120726
47907CB00014B/2314